John Douglas, William P. Bath

Seasonable Hints From an Honest Man

on the present important crisis of a new reign and a new parliament

John Douglas, William P. Bath

Seasonable Hints From an Honest Man
on the present important crisis of a new reign and a new parliament

ISBN/EAN: 9783337381028

Printed in Europe, USA, Canada, Australia, Japan

Cover: Foto ©Andreas Hilbeck / pixelio.de

More available books at **www.hansebooks.com**

SEASONABLE HINTS

FROM AN

HONEST MAN

ON THE PRESENT IMPORTANT CRISIS OF A

NEW REIGN

AND A

NEW PARLIAMENT.

Mihi indies magis animus accenditur, cum confidero quæ conditio vitæ futura fit, nifi nofmetipfos *vindicamus in libertatem*; nam, poftquam Refp. in *paucorum potentium* jus atque ditionem conceffit, femper illis *Reges* — vectigales effe——cæteri omnes, ftrenui, boni, nobiles, atque ignobiles, vulgus fuimus, fine gratia, fine auctoritate, his obnoxii quibus, fi *Refp. valeret*, formidini effemus.

SALLUST.

LONDON:

Printed for A. MILLAR, in the Strand.
M.DCC.LXI.
[Price One Shilling.]

SEASONABLE HINTS

FROM AN

HONEST MAN.

THERE is scarcely an individual in the nation, whose thoughts have not full employment given to them by the accession of a new monarch to the crown. The lowest as well as the highest ranks in the community, look upon themselves as interested in the great event. Our tradesmen and manufacturers view it as promoting or checking the profits of their respective branches of commerce and occupations. Others again, who join idleness to affluence, are fond of the prospect of a new reign, merely as it will open new scenes to gratify their gaping curiosity. Even the fair sex find themselves deeply concerned in the important crisis; and, perhaps, are puzzled, whether they have most reason to lament the sable uniformity of dress to which they are doomed; or to rejoice, that they have been already entertained with the melancholy splendor of a royal funeral, and are soon to be feasted with the pompous shew of a coronation.——If we step into the political world, the agitation and

A   hurry

hurry increafes; the hopes and fears of every one, who looks upon himfelf as connected with government, are all afloat ; ambition is at work in every corner; and from the fervile attendant in the drawing-room, to the ftately mini-fter in the council chamber, we find nothing but the eagernefs of expectation, or the appre-henfions of difappointment, painted in every face.

Amidft this ftrange tumult of bufinefs and of idlenefs, of condolance and congratulation, though I am too inconfiderable a member of the community, to think I have any right to mix as an actor, on the theatre of public life ; at the fame time, I have fo much vanity as to think myfelf confiderable enough to be indulged in giving my fentiments how I could wifh others may act. Not biaffed by the prejudices of party ; neither afraid of lofing a place, nor hoping to gain one, I feel myfelf impelled, al-moft irrefiftibly, in the infancy of his majefty's government, to throw into the hands of the public, with all the decency and moderation of the moft loyal fubject, yet with all the freedom and impartiality of the warmeft patriot, fome thoughts that have occurred to me on this moft important occafion. If I can fuggeft any thing that my co-incide with the fentiments of thofe who have power to carry my honeft wifhes in-to execution, I fhall think myfelf amply re-warded; if I fail in this, I fhall ftill hope that my readers, though they may call in queftion my abilities as a writer, will, at the fame time,

do

do juftice to my zeal as an *Englifhman*; and, at leaft, look upon this, my firft, and I believe laft attempt, as an author, to be a proof of my fincere attachment to his majefty's perfon and government; and dictated from a heart that pants with an ardent zeal to fee *him* great, and his people *happy*.

Happy as it was, that providence extended the life of his late majefty, till a fucceffor arrived at an age that fpurns the fetters of a *regency*, and delivers the nation from the confufion incident to a minority; it is ftill greatly to be lamented, that his reign was not prolonged till he had compofed that ferment which now rages throughout Europe; that fo he might leave no other care to his royal grandfon, but the eafy and pleafing one of bleffing his fubjects, by cultivating the arts of foreign and domeftic peace. But alas! the acceffion of his prefent majefty hath happened at a bufy and perplexing crifis. He hath been forced to lay hold of the helm of ftate while the veffel is ftill toft by a violent ftorm; and, though not in danger of fhipwreck, liable to many accidents before fhe can be brought into a fafe harbour.

But it is not my intention to enlarge upon the difficulties of this fort, with which his majefty begins his reign. With regard to the war, and our behaviour towards our allies, there can be but one path to walk in; and when the method of conduct is agreed upon,

confe-

confequences, however difagreeable, will be lefs perplexing. Adherence to the, fame counfels by which the war hath hitherto been conducted, will ftill, it is to be hoped, produce happy effects ; and it muft be left to time, and to circumftances, to find out a proper means of reconciling the loffes of our allies on the continent of Europe, with our own advantages in America ; and of extricating them from the danger that threaten their poffeffions, without facrificing our own conquefts; conquefts purchafed at the expence of fo many millions ; which our enemies, we are certain, are unable to recover by force, and which therefore, cannot be loft but by weak negotiations.

What principally hath given rife to this my attempt as a writer, is my eagernefs to exprefs, in the moft public manner, my hopes and my wifhes that, to the neceffary difficulties, occafioned by the war, under which his majefty has mounted the throne, unneceffary ones may not be fuperadded, by the avarice or ambition of courtiers, by the claims and importunities of candidates for power and places; by the ftruggle of parties, and the competition of factions, each aiming to be the monopolizers of the royal favour, and forcing themfelves, if they can, into employments.

I am very fenfible of the great nicety of my fubject, but I fhall endeavour to treat it in fuch a manner, that every friend of the conftitution may be convinced of the rectitude of my intentions,

tions, and own that I am not altogether unworthy to be looked upon as one of thofe
boneft men, whofe affiftance his majefty has
called for from the throne:

Were it poffible for me to be conveyed, for a
few moments, to the clofet, under the form of
fome *Mentor*, I fhould think myfelf obliged by
every dictate of loyalty, and every counfel of
prudence, to recommend and enforce this moft
feafonable piece of advice;----to be upon the
guard againft the artful applications of every fet
of courtiers; and by a proper firmnefs to convince every one that we have a monarch on the
throne, who knowing that he reigns in the
hearts of an united people, is determined not to
refign himfelf to the infolent pretenfions of any
confederacy of minifters.

The importance and feafonablenefs of fuch
advice is felf-evident. For if any fuch confederacy fhould be forming, or already formed (though I cannot fuppofe any body fo
weak, or fo wicked as to engage in it) the
manner in which it is treated, at its firft appearance, will have very decifive confequences;
in fhort, it will, in a great meafure, determine, whether the prince upon the throne, is
to reign over a free and united people, with
that full extent of power which our well-poifed
government allows to the crown, or whether
he is to content himfelf with the fhadow of
royalty, while a fet of *undertakers* for his bufinefs, intercept his immediate communication
with his people, and make ufe of the legal pre-
rogatives

rogatives of their *master*, to eſtabliſh the illegal claims of fa&ious *oligarchy*.

It were no difficult task, perhaps, to draw a ridiculous enough picture of the groupes of candidates for court-favors, on ſuch occaſions as the preſent; and to deſcribe with that ludicrous ſeverity which it deſerves, the inſatiable thirſt of thoſe who, though they have been intoxicated, for years, with the moſt copious draughts of the cup of power, are ſtill ſo unreaſonable as to be craving for more, to the utter excluſion of numbers, who have an equal right to taſte it in their turn. But the ſcramble for power and places, which of late years hath been, as it were, the great aim of almoſt every one who approached the throne, and which I ſo ardently wiſh may not revive at this juncture, is more the object of grave ſentiment than of giddy ridicule. We may laugh at the private foibles of the great, but cannot help being ſhocked at their public corruption. They are fit ſubjects for the poet's ſatire, when we view them confederating at a *horſe race*, or a *gaming table*; but of the patriot's indignation, when we conſider their conduct in *public life*, and obſerve their factious combinations to lay violent hands on every lucrative employment; true to their own mercenary concerns, but regardleſs of the national intereſt; devoted to ſome miniſter, at whoſe levee they bow with ſervility; and ſcarcely owning an obligation to the royal hand, which decency obliges them to kiſs.

It muſt give every lover of his country real
ſatiſ-

satisfaction, that those eminent counsellors, who advised and conducted the present war, are continued in employment at this time, that they may not be deprived of the opportunity of displaying their abilities, in extricating the nation out of those difficulties and distresses, in which, during their counsels, it was first involved. But at the same time, I should be sorry to see any minister, or knot of ministers, permitted to grasp universal influence in *domestic business*, and forcing his majesty, at his first entrance upon government, to nominate to all the employments about his person, in his family, and in his revenues, not those whom he himself thinks worthiest and likes best, but those whom the confederated Party-leaders may think most likely to be dependent on themselves, and whom they may make use of as their instruments to extend their influence, nay, to perpetuate their power, in opposition to the royal inclination.

A king who would hope for a reign of consequence, and ease, must begin with such a steadiness of conduct, as may convince every one who approaches him, that he knows it is the duty of his ministers to depend on him, and has too much spirit to depend on his ministers. If he shews his inclination to continue particular persons, in high office, he must at the same time, shew his resolution to break all factious *connections* and *confederacies*.

A new king surrounded by a set of grasping courtiers, each aiming at the management of him, like a virgin beset by her lovers, must,
upon

upon occafion, be able to check their importu-nity, and fteadily fay, *No*. The judicious ufe of this fhort, but expreffive monofyllable, will fave a world of trouble, and be the only means of preferving his future honour and dignity. But if once it be difcovered, that he durft not fay this on one occafion, his independence will, on every occafion, be attacked, till, at laft, by re-peated compliances, he fees himfelf doomed, through his whole reign, to fuffer violence from every one who fhall have infolence enough to make the attempt.

In a word, if a monarch do not begin his fo-vereignty by fuch a conduct, as will let the can-didates for power fee, that he will not permit them to force it from him, he will at laft fee himfelf the fervant of his own fervants; the fountain of all honors, without being able to beftow any; with a right to difpofe of every office however great, without being allowed to name to any one of the loweft; and if ever he fhould endeavor to extricate himfelf out of this unhappy ftate, he will then learn, by dear-bought experience, that it is much eafier to preferve independence, than to throw off fub-jection; and that one moment of fteadinefs, at the beginning of his reign, would have faved him years of trouble and diftrefs, in the pro-grefs of it.

Thefe reflections have too folid a foundation in found policy to be controverted in general; but the particular application of them to the prefent ftate of affairs in this country, will, I forefee,

forefee, meet with oppofition. While they coincide with the fentiments of every honeft and independent perfon in the nation, they may perhaps be difagreeable to certain individuals, who having long basked themfelves in the warm funfhine of a court, may, at laft, think they have a right to contract, within their own narrow fphere, every fpark of that luminary of majefty, which was intended to diffufe light and heat to the numerous and wide-extended objects capable of receiving its influence.——— To talk of the independency of the crown, on its own fervants, to fuch perfons, will have the air of a new and dangerous doctrine; and we fhall hear them, no doubt, (concealing, with their ufual modefty, their private views, under the appearance of public virtue) urge the neceffity of the king's fubmitting to give up the management of his affairs, and the exclufive difpofal of all his employments, to fome minifter, or fet of minifters, who, by uniting together, and backed by their numerous dependents, may be able to carry on the meafures of government.

This ftrange doctrine having been but too fafhionable of late years, and, in confequence of it, confederated minifters having but too frequently, in the former reigns, offered the moft unwarrantable violence to majefty, I- fhall think myfelf very laudably employed, if, without meaning to attack individuals for what is paft, and ftudious only to guard againft what is

B   wrong

wrong for the future, I offer some seasonable reflections on this great and national subject.

It used to be looked upon as the perfection of the *English* government, that the supreme power is divided between the three estates of the kingdom; but according to the doctrine of the above-mentioned monopolizers of places, the present distribution of power is a faulty one; and, in order to correct this fault, a cabal of ministers must be allowed to erect themselves into a fourth estate, to check, to controul, to influence, nay, to enslave the other three. If the advocates for governing by such a system would speak out, they must admit this to be the principle on which all their politics proceed; and when once they have been brought to own that it is their intention to annihilate every constitutional power in the British legislature, by the influence of a private unconstitutional association of party leaders, we shall then have much the same sort of esteem for them, that we should have for the confederacy of a few lawyers, who could have the modesty to assert, that in order to carry on the business of Westminster-Hall, as it ought to be, the whole of it should pass through their hands only, and they be allowed to bully the judges, and to bribe the juries into such decisions as they shall dictate.

If ministers should insist, that none but their dependents must be put into employments, upon pretence that if those employments be conferred on others, the just designs of the king will

will meet with oppofition, what is this but to
fay, in other words, that private intereft, avarice, or ambition, are the only motives that
guide them in their conduct, with regard to
the public; and that they will oppofe thofe very
meafures they now fupport, unlefs they be allowed to pay themfelves for fupporting them?
Can there be any thing fo unworthy of Eng-
lifhmen, men of honor, and good fubjects, as
an open avowal of fuch fcandalous combinations, which appear to be formed upon this
fingle principle of ferving the crown, only for
their own convenience, and of oppofing its
meafures, for every reafon, but a conviction
that they are wrong? Can there, therefore, be
a lover of his country, who would not wifh to
fee the prince upon the throne fet all fuch confederacies, if any fhould arife, at defiance?
And can there be the leaft doubt, that the nation, in general, would lift itfelf on his fide, if
any fet of all-grafping courtiers fhould have the
infolence to make attempts on his independence? The Englifh are too fober and fenfible
a people to prefer the dark and arbitrary influence of *Ariftocracy,* to the known legal claims
of a limited *Monarchy.* Their fovereign, therefore, will never want friends to ftand by him,
when the competition is not between prerogative and liberty, but between king and minifters: and as a king in this country will find *no
party* ftrong enough to fupport his government,
when once the body of the nation fees him do
wrong, fo, on the other hand, if he does what
is right, fafe in the affections of a great and ge-

nerous

nerous people, no faction need ever appear so formidable, in its influence and number of dependents, as to force him to give way to their insolent attempts to perpetuate their power, in opposition to his inclination.

To hear some folks talk of the necessity the crown is under to submit to the direction and management of confederated ministers, one would imagine, that the times of the *old barons* were revived, when by their feudal superiorities, military vassals, and numerous retainers, they could, at any time, if they united together, measure swords with their sovereign: but thank God, those times have been long at an end, and the great men of this country have no means of making themselves considerable, and of procuring dependents, but such as the crown furnishes them with, by intrusting them with the direction of that influence which is its own, which may be resumed at pleasure, and which whenever it is resumed, must leave the greatest leader of a ministerial confederacy, as insignificant as he was before thought formidable. If there have been instances in modern times, that seem to contradict my assertion, this hath not arisen from real power in the subject, but from weak timidity and ill judged compliance in the crown. An indolent master, who gives up the entire management of his fortune to a favourite steward, permitting him, for a number of years, to appoint or to displace all his domestic servants, to raise their wages, or to grant them annuities out of the estate, without ever controuling

trouling his intentions, or calling him to account ; fuch a perfon as this, it is natural to
fuppofe, will find his fteward's influence more
extenfive than his own, in the family ; becaufe
the individuals, who compofe it, fee no proba-
bility that he ever means to extricate himfelf
from bondage. But when once they are convinced he rea.ly intends to difmifs his govern-
nor, and to do his own bufinefs, the domef-
ticks will then find it their intereft to be dutiful ; or if they fhould be fo far impofed upon,
as to be induced to join in a confederacy, to
oppofe their mafter's intended change, one
who gives good wages, need not fear to get a
new fet of fervants, and therefore can have no
reafon to bear with infults from the old ones.

The application of this to the cafe before
us, is obvious. Our kings have fometimes given fuch unlimited indulgence to their minifters, that thofe put into employments, fcarcely ever looked beyond the minifters to own an
obligation. The natural confequence of this
was, that minifters employed the influence of
the crown to make it fubmit to themfelves ;
and having once acquired a number of dependents, purchafed by doleing out the king's
bounty, they had the infolence to urge the
number of their dependents, as a reafon why
the king fhould bow to their minifterial om-
nipotence.—A prince who can be intimidated
by the cabals of thofe who derive all their importance and influence from the unlimited
difpofal they have had of his favours, fcarcely
                                        deferves

deferves pity, becaufe he has the means of liberty, but wants fpirit to affert it. Let him once fhew that he is determined to be looked upon as mafter, and he will foon feel he will be refpected as fuch; and if any over-grown minifter fhould think this an encroachment on his office, and begin to fhew his inclination to diftrefs government, which he no longer can manage without controul, he will foon find that his fuppofed friends were only the friends of his power, and will continue firm to him no longer than while he has poffeffion of the means of gratifying them. In the age we live in there are but few individuals, I am fure there are but few retainers of a court, fo little attentive to their own intereft, as to forget that the crown is permanent, and adminiftrations temporary; that a king is fuch all the days of his life, and that minifters exift only by his pleafure. To fuppofe, therefore, that a dif-carded leader of party, fhould find his myrmi-dons willing to continue faithful to his ftandard, when it is fet up in oppofition to that of the king, is to fuppofe them capable of a conduct to which their leader himfelf muft know they are entire ftrangers.

The reader will readily fuppofe that thefe reflexions are made without a view to *particular facts*, or without a fufpicion that any mi-nifterial cabals are now forming againft the crown; and that they are thrown out here only to fhew, in cafe fuch cabals fhould be formed, at any future period, that they never

can

can be formidable to a prince, who knows the extent of his own importance, and is refolved not to facrifice it to the ambition of a few fubjects.

Indeed, in one cafe, and in one cafe only, can the fovereign of this country ever fear the refentment of a difgufted minifter, or of a difcarded party ; and that is, when a plaufible pretence for oppofition can be taken up, and the bulk of the nation induced to intereft itfelf in it, and to believe that it was formed by the leaders of it, not on account of their difappointments in the ftruggle for power, but on account of their honeft difapprobation of the public plan of government.——But I think I may venture to give it as my opinion, that, were it poffible to conceive there could be, at prefent, an intention in any combination of men to oppofe government, they could not find fuch a pretence for oppofition, as they could lay hold of with any appearance of decency, or hopes of fuccefs.

When I fay this, I am not ignorant of the public diftreffes, and of the uneafinefs every real *patriot* muft feel, and exprefs, when he fees this poor country bleeding at every vein ; borrowing annually twelve millions, and fpending, at leaft, twenty! already incumbered with a debt of one hundred and twenty millions! and this amazing load ftill daily increafing !—--
When the lover of his country reflects coolly

on

on this its prefent fituation, the moft melancholy reflections muft fucceed to the exultation of
conqueft. But whither will thefe reflections
lead him? Not furely to charge our diftreffes
to his majefty's account, who found us in fuch
a ftate, that we cannot retreat from our enormous expences, without ignominy, though
God knows, how long we may be able to per-
fevere in them!

If then the diftreffes of the public furnifh
no object, at prefent, for the oppofition of the
patriot, who has had no fhare in promoting
the meafures that have fo involved us, much
lefs can they be made a handle to inflame the
nation, by any of thofe who were in power
in the late reign. Can fuch a perfon, in cafe
he fhould fail in acquiring that fhare of influence in the cabinet, he formerly might have,
ftand up, with any confiftency of character,
to throw the firft ftone at meafures, entered
into during his own adminiftration, and for
which himfelf and his affociates were anfwer-
able? Could it be borne to hear him expati-
ate on the immenfe increafe of the national
debt ; on the too great fhare we have taken in
the continental war, and on the glaring want
of occonomy with which it has been conducted?-----No, the honeft, the independent part
of the nation (the only part of it that government can wifh to pleafe, or fear to difoblige)
would be able to trace, under this veil of patriotifm, the real character of difappointed ambition,

bition ; and would difregard the barking of this ftate *Cerberus,* whofe mouth, they know, can, at any time, be ftopt, by throwing him his fop.

But I ftate a cafe which I am confident will not happen. For though we had not a fuffi-cient fecurity from the experience we have had of the difinterefted loyalty of thofe who have of late been accuftomed to power, that they are incapable of engaging in any combinations to diftrefs government, there could not be the leaft reafon to fulpect that any of them could be fo *imprudent,* as to attempt it, at a time, when they muft be confcious they ftand great-ly in need of the protection of the crown, that their former adminiftration may not be remem-bered to their difadvantage. In a word, fhould ill-informed patriotifm, or mercenary ambi-tion, ever think of charging on this reign the bloodfhed which may enfue, and the additional millions of debt, which the prefent war may ftill make neceffary, his majefty may well be defended by faying, that he fuffers from the difmal confequences of meafures entered into by former adminiftrations; and the words of Shakefpeare may be well applied on this occa-fion :

Shake not thy gorey locks at me,
Thou canft not fay that I did it.

As I cannot figure to myfelf a more unhap-py fituation than that of a Prince, who, with

C   all

all the abilities requisite for his station, and with all the inclination to support his own virtuous principles, and his independence, finds himself reduced to the mortifying necessity of submitting to be dictated to by a cabal of ambitious subjects, it is with singular pleasure I have been able to remark, that the circumstances under which his majesty begins his reign, give us a prospect, that no aristocratic usurpations will be attempted, or if they were attempted, that they would prove as unsuccessful, as they are odious.

But however flattering these circumstances are, it is not impossible that unconstitutional restraints on majesty may again be attempted by associated ministers. It will not, therefore, be unseasonable, to look back a little to those times, when we know government was engrossed by such ambitious leaders of party; and without exaggerating their insolence, and the fatal consequences which the public felt from their plan of administration, we shall be able to draw such a picture of it, as will strike every lover of his king and country with indignation, and make us unite with heart and hand to prevent its revival.

I shall consider the reign of confederated statesmen in two lights; first, as it offered personal indignities to the king; and secondly, as it naturally gave birth to such arts of government as were subversive of public liberty, and destructive of the constitution.-----The history of

of this country, in times not very remote, will
enable me, alas! to give but too many melancholy proofs of each of the above particulars.

Though the plan of fettering majefty in the
chains of party, was at leaft coeval with the
acceffion of the royal family ; minifters, at firft,
could not guefs how far they might venture
to pufh their ufurped influence. Our hiftory,
fince the times of the *barons*, had furnifhed few
or no inftances of *oligarchical* reftraint put upon
the crown ; it required time and experience,
therefore, to model this new fyftem of modern
politics. And furely nothing but experience
could have proved it to be poffible, that a time
fhould ever happen, when the dignity of the
king could be trampled upon without regard
to decency : and when minifters might prefume
to carry their infolence fo far as to fet their mafter at defiance, and to govern in fpite of him.
------ I need not enter into many particulars,
to enable my readers to guefs, to what period
of our hiftory I now allude.

The court cafuifts in the reign of *Charles* I.
in order to prevail upon him to pafs the attain-
der of Lord *Strafford*, found out a curious diftinction between his private confcience, as a
man, and his public one, as a king. Some
minifters, in a more modern reign, feem to
have taken the hint from this ; when they
practifed a doctrine, which fhewed it to be
their refolution, that the king fhould be forc-

ed,

ced, in 'the moſt indecent manner, to diveſt himſelf of the feelings of a man; and in order to have the ambition of a few ſubjects gratified, ſhould not be permitted to reſent perſonal in-ſults, and indignities.

What ſhould we think of ſoldiers who threaten their general to abandon his ſtandards, when the enemy is in ſight, mutinying, not for want of pay, but in hopes to extort from him unreaſonable gratifications? What opi-nion could we have of a crew of ſailors, who, when their ſhip was in danger of ſinking, ſhould refuſe to ſtand to the pump, and threaten to go off in the long-boat, unleſs the maſter ſhould ſubmit to be put in irons, and allow them to divide the cargo? or to uſe an illuſ-tration perhaps ſtill more ſimilar to the tranf-action now alluded to, what notion could we have of the characters of a ſet of domef-tics, who, in order to force an indulgent maſ-ter to ſubmit to them, ſhould infiſt on his dif-miſſing every friend from his houſe; require him to take into his family ſome of their own dependents, who had perſonally uſed him ill, and whoſe preſence might be neceſſary to aſ-ſiſt them in enſlaving him; and finding him averſe to compliance, ſhould take occaſion, when they ſaw his houſe on fire, to threaten, in a body, they would abandon him, at that dangerous conjuncture, unleſs he yielded im-mediately to all their inſolent demands? ------ ------The queſtions I now ſtate, but faintly de-ſcribe the odious circumſtances of an *aſſociation*

of

of minifters, within the memory of many, but exactly when, I won't fay, who, finding that though they had forced their fovereign to fubmit to many mortifying indignities and galling conceffions, he had too delicate a fenfe of honor not to make refiftance againft fome of their demands, had recourfe to an act of factious infolence, of which no preceding part of our hiftory furnifhed an example. For, at a time when every honeft fubject ought to have had full employment in foothing the diftreffes of majefty, and in defending the tottering throne; when faction fhould have fufpended its ambitious intrigues, to oppofe daring difaffection, and too fuccefsful rebellion; at that very inftant, the nation faw with amazement a *formal confederacy* entered into by the king's fervants, affociating to refign, in a body, in hopes that their unhappy fovereign, alarmed to be abandoned at fuch a crifis of public danger, might be induced to comply with every demand of their infolent ambition, which, hitherto, he had refufed to gratify.

If my memory fails me not, it was not much above a week after a fecond victory gained over the king's forces by the rebels, that this rebellion in the cabinet broke out; a rebellion which impartial pofterity will, perhaps, look upon as equally *unnatural* with that of the rebel lords, who were then in arms againft the crown, whofe open treafons could fcarcely exceed in guilt, the fecret cabals of the *affociated band of minifters*, who, by their conduct on
this

this occasion, convinced the world that it was the principal article in their political creed, that they had a right to force the king to constitute them his council of regency, and that the throne was not to be supported, unless the prince who sat upon it consented to bear their yoke.

Happy had it been for the prince, on whose independence this amazing attempt was made; happy had it been for the public, if he had thrown himself upon his parliament then sitting, for protection, against the insolence of a set of men, whom he had gratified with power, loaded with riches, and invested with honors! Had he done this, powerful as the confederacy might think themselves, the English generosity would have fired; the cause of injured majesty would have become the cause of a loyal public; and those ministers, whose undutifulness had only risen from excessive indulgence, would have learnt, that a king of England need only *feel* his own consequence to make those feel it who insult him.

The transaction above referred to is pregnant with so many odious circumstances, that I should have been glad, for the honor of our country, to have drawn a veil over it. But my argument naturally led me to take notice of it; and every candid reader must admit that I have touched the wound with the gentlest hand; and with the single and honest intention, of warning every future confederacy of party-lead-

crs

ers, to avoid such personal insults on the sovereign, as *history* must relate with severe ani-
madversion, *patriotism* read with indignation,
and *candor* itself can scarcely endeavour to ex-
tenuate. It was the fashion of the times we
have been speaking of, to use such factious methods of acquiring and preserving the power;
and much is to be said to lessen the guilt of
those who are linked with a party, and bound,
as it were, in honor (at least thinking themselves so) to attempt things as an aggregate body, which, as individuals, they perhaps dis-
approved of, at the very time, and which, certainly, they could not but condemn, as soon as
the violence of party zeal subsided, and cool
reflexion was permitted to operate on probity
and good sense.

If ministerial combinations to engross power,
and to invade the closet, have produced such
personal insults on the *king*, the consequences of
such attempts, with regard to the public, were
equally odious. For truth obliges me to con-
fess, that however favorable to national freedom
the true genuine principles of *whiggism* be, some
individuals of that denomination, (who, in times
happily at an end, got possession of the royal
family) were the great promoters, if not the
first introducers, of such a plan of wicked policy, as had a natural tendency to sap the firm
foundation of British liberty, and to destroy the
independence of the constitution.

The

The charge I now bring may seem severe; but the facts, on which it is built, are notorious.----Such is the happy diftribution of supreme power in this country, that the sovereign finds it his intereft to purfue no meafures but fuch as are agreeable to the reprefentatives of the people; and the neceffity of obtaining par-. liamentary concurrence has increafed fince the revolution; from which period, by feparating the civil lift from the other charges of government, annual feffions muft be held, and annual fupplies granted. Minifters, therefore, who wanted to force themfelves into employments at court, faw that they fhould gain their point, if they could convince the fovereign that they had the power over parliament. But how could any particular fet of men acquire fuch a power? It was impoffible that the whole body of the people, in this great country, fhould concur in enflaving their fovereign and themfelves, to any junto of their fellow fubjects; and it was obvious that a parliament *chofen freely,* and compofed of gentlemen of real property, whofe inclination it would be to *vote freely,* were not likely to act the defpicable part of tools to a narrow party-cabal of ambitious courtiers.

In this fituation, therefore, there was no alternative; the fcheme of putting the fovereign into the leading-ftrings of party muft be abandoned, or elfe fuch methods put in practice, as might check the freedom of election, and procure fuch a parliament as might fupport a particular

cular set of ministers. The real disaffection that existed at the accession of George the First, furnished those who then got possession of the closet, with a specious pretence to employ secretly the court influence upon certain important occasions; and having once prevailed upon the king to look upon such *secret* influence, as necessary for the security of his family, they knew it would answer a more immediate purpose to themselves, by giving them the means of perpetuating their own power; a point, in their opinion, not too dearly purchased, by a most enormous expence of public money, † and by establishing venality and corruption into a system, as necessary engines of government.

To consider the English constitution in theory, its stability would be supposed to arise from parliament. But parliaments, when once they become appendages of administration, must open the widest door to slavery. In this case, they become a mere *state engine* in the hands of the minister, to *stamp* a value on the basest metal, and to give every bad measure the sanction of national consent. And no chains are so heavy as those which we put on ourselves; for we shall bear from our representatives, what

† From 1707 to 1717, the whole amount of the money issued on account of the secret services, was only 337960 l. 4 s. 5 d. But, from 1731 to 1741, the same number of years, how amazingly it increased?. For, within this last period, there was issued, under the same head, 1453400 l. 6 s. See the report of the secret committee.

D   prero-

prerogative, openly exerted, never will venture to put in practice.

Happy is it for the conftitution, that fuch
over-ruling influence over parliaments has ceafed! Had the fyftem of modelling them, by minifterial lifts, and minifterial interpofition,conti-
nued, parliaments, by degrees, would have loft
their dignity; the landed gentlemen would
have found it impoffible to get feats; and brok-
ers from Change Alley (who pay no taxes for
their money) and placemen from the treafury
(for whofe benefit taxes are paid) would have,
in time, had the honour of paffing votes to lay
annual burthens on the landed property, in
which they themfelves are but little concerned.
And if ever this time had arrived, every lover
of his country would have wifhed to fee an
end put to thofe very affemblies, which by
keeping up the empty forms of the conftitution,
would only have haftened the lofs of real liberty; and verified the wife obfervation, that England can never be undone but by a parliament.

If the reign of monopolizing ftatefmen be
deftructive of liberty, and of the independence
of parliament, no wonder that it fhould be attended with other collateral mifchiefs. In fuch
times, we need not be furprized if the true
interefts of the kingdom, with regard to foreign
affairs, be neglected, by thofe who look upon
every object as fubordinate to that of perpetuating their own power. And, with regard to
domeftic policy, there can be but little chance
to

o fee much attention to what is *right* in a public view, when private intereſt is the avowed principle of thoſe who have power. Through every department of government, thoſe perſons only will be preferred, who are moſt likely to do the miniſter's buſineſs, without regarding how unfit they are to be truſted with that of the nation. The favours of power will be proſtituted to the moſt profligate ; and it will be the ſum of all merit, to have intereſt in ſome borough, or to be related to thoſe who have. — In a word, the ſpirit, the morals, the religion, the reputation, and importance of the nation will decay, and the *body politic* droop under univerſal *corruption*.

Surely I ſhall be pardoned for the warmth with which I have expreſſed myſelf, in ſpeaking of the times when government was ſeized upon by a confederacy of miniſters ; and every friend of monarchy, every lover of liberty, every one not bred up in the ſchool of miniſterial corruption, will heartily join me, in my ardent wiſhes to ſee this ſyſtem for ever exploded ; in a word, to ſee his majeſty lay hold of the uncommon advantages, with which, as we have obſerved above, he aſcends the throne, to keep himſelf free from its dominion.

But why ſhould I content myſelf with expreſſing my wiſhes on this head? ---- We can already appeal to facts which give us well-grounded hopes, that the ſovereign now upon the throne will adopt thoſe principles, which

appear

appear so neceffary, to make his reign glorious, and his people happy.

Here then let me congratulate my fellow-subjects, on the pleasing profpects which already open to our view. In this infancy of his majesty's government, he hath conducted himfelf, in fuch a manner, as gives us just grounds to form the highest ideas, both of his good dispositions and of his abilities; to expect that this will be a reign of dignity and importance, a reign in which the ministers will depend on the crown, and not the crown on the ministers; in fhort, a reign in which the hateful and worn-out distinctions of party will be abolished, and government carried on, without having recourfe to the mifchievous arts of corruption, and without reviving the odious tyranny of ministerial dictators.

Such hath been the infolence of former administrations, that a king of England hath frequently feen himfelf unable to confer the smalleft employment, unlefs on the recommendation, and with the confent of his *ministers*. If I may be allowed to credit *fome* facts, which every one of my readers muft have heard, ----- it should feem that the long-wished for time is come, when fubjects may expect to receive favours from the crown, without owing the obligation to all-directing ministers.

But it is not merely from this circumstance, that we hope for a new *æra*; for we fee that
his

his majesty is resolved to put himself at the head of all his subjects, by abolishing all the distinctions of party, by accepting with paternal affection the assistance of *every honest man*, to support the throne; and, as a mark of his royal confidence, placing in the most honorable stations, near his own person, some, who have not surely owed their places to ministerial importunity, because they have always opposed ministerial influence.

The circumstances attending this most important measure give us room to hope for the most flattering consequences. Some few of the *proscribed party*, have, indeed, in former reigns, been put into employment; but, though individuals were gratified, the party still remained in opposition. Now, every thing is different. Those of that denomination now taken into employment, are followed by the whole body of their friends to the royal presence, where they mix, unplaced and unpensioned, with the numerous throng of dutiful subjects, and give us just reason to exult with Shakespear, that

England never did, and never shall
Lye at the proud foot of a conqueror,
But when it did first help to wound itself .
Now these her princes *are come home again,*
Come the three corners of the world in
    arms,
And we shall shock them.

But,

But, has not this very meafure given an
alarm? Has it not been thought a hardſhip on
thoſe who have been enriched with all the re-
wards of government, theſe fifty years, to have
ſo much as one employment given away, from
their party? This language, we are certain,
cannot be held amongſt miniſters themſelves,
though it may be faſhionable amongſt their
humble dependents; who have always the *loaves
and fiſhes in their eye.* But I would recommend it
to ſuch gentlemen, to moderate their reſentment
on this occaſion. For it is ten to one, that if
they ſhew it any where, but in their own private *juntos,* they may be addreſſed in the words
of Horace;

*Luſiſti ſatis; ediſti ſatis, atque bibiſti:
Tempus abire tibi eſt; ----*

You have rioted long enough, gentlemen, at
the expence of the public; you have had places
and penſions, and jobs, and contracts, and ſub-
ſcriptions, in abundance: --- it is time now for
you to think you have had your full ſhare of
lucre, and to make room for others who have
been fleeced to gorge you with plunder.

It is ſcarcely poſſible to avoid being ludicrous
when we take notice of the inſolent pretenſions
and complaints of the mob of placemen (for
their leaders do not ſurely join in the cry) on the
alarm that the bottom of government is to be
widened. I wiſh ſome body would take the trouble

ble of making a computation how much money has been received by a placeman who has, we will suppose, a salary of three thousand pounds a year, and then set it against the money that has been paid by a country gentleman, for the same number of years, as taxes on an estate of the same value ; and then see whether it can be borne, that the same persons should be constantly continued in employment, while all equally offer their service. I am but very aukward at such computations, but I think it will not be difficult to balance accounts between the placeman and country gentleman.-----I have heard, above twenty years ago, that a proprietor of land paid above thirteen shillings *per* pound in taxes to the public. The many additional loads laid upon us since that time, induce me to think that, at present, he pays full fifteen shillings. Nor will this computation be thought very wide from the mark, by any one who will reflect, that besides reckoning the heavy sums paid in hard money, we include in this calculation the endless variety of taxes that raise the price of every convenience, nay, of every necessary of life, and encrease our expence insensibly, in every article we have occasion to purchase.-----If we proceed then, upon this foundation, we shall find that a country gentleman, with a rent-roll of 3000 l. *per ann.* will have paid in taxes, in the course of twenty years, at least *forty five thousand pounds* : while a placeman, who is paid 3000 *l. per annum*, as a salary, during the same period, will have put into his pocket,

ket *fixty thoufand pounds* of the public money. Can there be equity in fuch glaring inequality? And can it be ftrange, that there fhould be uneafineffes and difcontents in the kingdom, while the many are *impóverifhed*, to enrich the few? A prince therefore cannot begin his reign with a more endearing meafure, than to fatisfy the body of his faithful fubjects, whofe burthens are fo grievous, that no particular fet of men is to expect to be exempted from feeling the weight of them; while others equally worthy of his protection, are doomed to be *hewers of wood*, and *drawers of water*, with nothing to boaft of, but the comfortable employment of paying exorbitant taxes: taxes! too great a part of the amount of which, they have feen employed to carry on that fyftem of monopoly, by which they themfelves were oppreffed, and to furnifh the means of luxury and profufion to their oppreffors.

When the private intereft of a few individuals is affected, we frequently fee that they have art enough to get their caufe to be looked upon as the caufe of a whole party. I fhould be forry if this happened to be the cafe at prefent; and yet, we have been told, that, becaufe a few *tories* have got places, attempts have been made to induce the *whigs* to confider this as an attack on their whole body: but if the *whigs* can be fo far deluded as to believe this, it will give us a remarkable proof, that *party is the madnefs of the many, for the gain of the few.* For does
any

any candid and intelligent man serioufly believe, that at this time of day, there subfifts
any party diftinction amongft us, that is not
merely nominal ? Are not the *tories* friends of
the *royal family* ? Have they not long ago laid
afide their averfion to the diffenters ? Do they
not think the toleration and eftablifhment, both
neceffary parts of the conftitution ? And can
a *whig* diftinguifh thefe from his own principles ? Muft not, therefore, every honeft man
fee and confefs, that the cry againft widening
the bottom of government, is propagated by
fome, who, finding their own views of ambition or gain affected by this meafure, endeavor to render it odious amongft the body of
the party, who otherways would have feen no
reafon to be alarmed, even in point of private
intereft ? For all that the *tories* poffibly can
hope for, or expect, is, that a few marks of confidence may be given them at prefent, as a
proof, that the *profcription* is at an end, and as an
earneft, that in the future difpofal of court fa-
vors, when there are vacancies by deaths and
not by removals, they will ftand an equal
chance of being taken notice of, with the reft
of his Majefty's good fubjects. And here I may
ask; has fo much as a fingle *whig* been difplaced, to make room for a *tory* fucceffor ? Have
not the few places conferred on the formerly
excluded party, been fuch as his Majefty has
created, in his own bed-chamber, by increafing the number of his fervants ? Why therefore
fhould there be complaints, where there is fo little foundation ? Indeed, the thing fpeaks for

E.   itfelf,

itfelf. The ground of the uneafinefs is not that any *whig* has been difplaced, but that a nation of *whigs*, as we may now juftly be called, muft ceafe for the future to be governed by the narrow maxims of faction.

If it muft give every friend of the *royal family* a fincere fatisfaction, to fee the *profcription* of the *tories.* ended ; there is another equally pleafing profpect now opened to our view,---we may hope, that the days of undue influence over *parliaments* never can be *revived.*

The original pretence for iffuing money for purpofes not publicly avowed, was to prevent the *jacobite* party from prevailing in their elections : but the extinction of *jacobitifm* has put an end to that pretence.

If money were to be iffued at prefent, for the purpofes we fpeak of, whom could it be employed againft ?---Againft gentlemen who have given convincing proofs of their loyalty to the prefent royal family ; have heartily concurred to fupport government in parliament, and have offered their fervices at court, in the prefent reign, which fervices his majefty has been pleafed to accept. And fhall it be fuppofed, that gentlemen, who have been thought worthy by the king, to be placed in the moft honorable ftations in his family, fhould be oppofed by the minifters, as unworthy to be admitted into

into parliament ?---The suppofition is highly ab-
furd ; and, therefore, I muft beg leave to exprefs my disbelief of a report, very current, *that
when a great perfonage was applied to, to know
how much money fhould be iffued, for a certain important purpofe*, his anfwer was, *Not a farth-
ing*.

I make no doubt, fuch an application would
have met with fuch an anfwer ; but, I cannot
believe the application was ever made, and am
inclined to think, that the report muft have
been raifed by fome enemy of the great minifter who has the direction of money matters:
For to fuppofe that the *corruption* of former days
fhould be revived, when the reafon given for
its being firft introduced has entirely ceafed,
would, in effect, be to tell us, that we are never more to have an independent parliament.
If at fuch a time as this, when the only con-
tention throughout the kingdom, is, who fhall
give the ftrongeft proofs of attachment to the
king, the people of England are not thought fit
to be trufted with the free exercife of their right
to choofe their reprefentatives, this would be a
public declaration to all the world, that they
never ought to be trufted with it, and that *corruption* is to be ingrafted into our conftitution.
But furely this doctrine cannot poffibly be a-
dopted by the great minifter whofe name has
been made ufe of on this occafion. He has by
his paft conduct fhewn, that he deferves no fuch
reproach, and we have no reafon to fear, that
one who did not exert an undue minifterial influence,

fluence, in choofing the parliament now fitting, fhould have the leaft intention to exert it at the enfuing election. He has befides, other things to think of at prefent, more adapted to his office, and to the exigencies of the ftate; and, inftead of examining lifts of boroughs, and qualifications of candidates, he will be better employed in examining into the exorbitant contingencies of our German and American commiffaries and contractors, that there may not be a deficiency of above *four millions*, befides the *twelve* that are borrowed, for the fervice of next campaign.

The above reafons feem fufficient to induce any one to disbelieve the report of money asked and refufed; but I think there may be fomething *ftill* ftronger faid on the fubject.------- The minifter who could propofe to the crown, at prefent, to employ fecret-fervice-money, for domeftic purpofes relative to the enfuing election, could not make fuch a propofal without betraying a fecret he had better keep to himfelf,----I mean, that he defires the *fingering* of the public money, only to ferve his own private views of ambition. Every candidate throughout the kingdom, at the approaching period, will be the king's friend, and willing to fupport his government. It is indifferent to the crown who is chofen, whether it be John or Thomas, when both of them are equally good fubjects. A minifter, therefore, who fhould think of employing the money of the crown, at this conjuncture, to oppofe and fupport particular

ticular candidates, would fhew plainly that he means not fo much to do the king's bufinefs, as his own, by increafing the number of his *own* immediate dependents, and forming a party who may owe their *obligations* to himfelf fingly, and encourage him to grafp univerfal influence, in fpite of the royal inclination. Far be it from me to fufpect, there can be any minifters at prefent, who have fuch views; but I am fure, if they fhould defire to be allowed to employ money for fecret domeftic purpofes, it would look as if they had.

I am very fenfible, that there are many well-meaning perfons who feem to think, that without *corruption*, there might be danger apprehended from *Democratical* encroachments on prerogative.----But they who are really ftruck with the above objection; certainly forget that tho' the wings of *prerogative* have been clipt, the *influence* of the crown is greater than ever it was in any period of our hiftory. For when we confider, in how many boroughs the government has the voters at its command; when we confider the vaft body of perfons employed in the collection of the revenue in every part of the kingdom; the inconceivable number of placemen, and candidates for places in the *cuftoms*, in the *excife*, in the *poft office*, in the *dock yards*, in the *ordnance*, in the *falt office*, in the *ftamps*, in the *navy* and *victualing* offices, and in a variety of other departments; when we confider again the extenfive influence of the *money corporations, fubfcription jobbers*, and

con-

contractors; the endlefs dependence created by the obligations conferred on the bulk of the gentlemen's families throughout the kingdom, who have relations preferred, or waiting to be preferred, in our *navy*, and numerous *ftanding army*; when, I fay, we confider how wide, how binding a dependence on the crown is created by the above enumerated particulars, no lover of monarchy need fear any bad confequences from fhutting up the Exchequer at elections; efpecially, when to the endlefs means the crown has of influencing the votes of the *electors*, we add the vaft number of employments, which the fafhion of the times makes the *elected* defirous of, and for the obtaining which, they muft depend upon the crown.

But, I believe, I have expreffed myfelf improperly, when I fpoke of the influence of the crown; for to fay the truth, we may have obferved from experience, that in proportion as the crown had the power of *obliging*, minifters, by being permitted to affume the univerfal direction of all thofe who had been *obliged*, have too frequently been enabled to make ufe of the dependents on the crown, to bring it into fubjection to themfelves; and at the fame time, while they became formidable to the prince, they have had it in their power to make attempts on the liberties of the people. For when the crown-influence lies difperfed in its feveral diftinct channels; when every placeman, or public officer, is left at full freedom to vote for the candidate he likes beft; numerous

ous as thefe gentlemen are throughout the kingdom, they never can be fuppofed united in any fcheme to hurt public liberty. But when they are to pafs in mufter before a firft minifter; when they are taught to look upon him as their commander in chief, and know that difobedience to his orders will be conftrued *mutiny*, and punifhed as fuch; when inftruftions are difpatched by the paliamentary undertaker, to every fervant of the crown to fupport and oppofe particular candidates; when every placeman, from the *excife-man* and *tide-waiter* up to the *commiffioner* and *courtier*, has a minifterial lift delivered to him; when the influence of the crown, I fay, is thus moulded into one connefted mafs, and trufted to the direftion of a fingle minifter, What objeft can be ftrong enough to refift its force? And how fatally will it operate in deftroying the independence of parliament, even though the *flood-gate* of *corruption* fhould be ftopt?

If the interpofition of a lord of parliament, in any particular eleftion, be carefully provided againft (as we know it is by the ftanding orders of the houfe of commons) as inconfiftent with the conftitution, how much more daring an attack is it upon the very effence of parliament, to fee a minifter prefume to *undertake*, not for one or two members only, in places where he has a natural intereft, but for hundreds of reprefentatives, in boroughs fcarcely known to him by name? What notion can any one have of the freedom of elections, if the writs for a

new

new parliament iſſued by the crown, are ac-
companied by private inſtructions from a miniſter, like ſo many *congè d'elires*, which muſt
implicitly be obeyed?

I think it would be no difficult matter to draw
a pretty ridiculous repreſentation of a firſt miniſter, iſſuing his orders to the numerous ſtand-
ing army of placemen, and making out a liſt
of members for a new parliament: and I would
recommend it to Mr. Hogarth, to try his fer-
tile imagination, in a drawing for a *political print*
on this ſubject. I would have the *great man*, ſur-
rounded by all his truſty dependents and clerks,
drawn, ſeated at a table, on which ſhould be
placed, variety of books and papers, diſtin-
guiſhed each by its proper label. Here we
might read, *liſts of voters* under the *exciſe*, the
cuſtoms, the *war office*, &c. &c. *liſts* of ſheriffs
and returning officers; and exact accounts of
the ſtate of *admiralty* boroughs, *navy office* boroughs, *ordnance* boroughs, *cinque port* boroughs, *poſt office* boroughs, &c. &c.------Before
the *great undertaker* ſhould lie open a liſt of the
members laſt choſen, which he is to alter and
amend as he thinks proper. In this ſituation,
methinks, he will ſeem like ſome author, when
his devil has juſt brought him a freſh ſheet
from the preſs, to be corrected; and like him
too, he writes a *ſtet* againſt ſuch names as he
intends to be choſen again; D for a proſcribing
dele, againſt thoſe he intends to be left out;
and Q's, for farther information about others,
of whom he has ſome doubts. One of the
clerks

clerks who attended on fuch an occafion, (I am fure no body can guefs either at the minifter or clerk) told me, that there were certain myfte-rious letters againft almoft all the names in the lift; but the meaning of thefe, he faid, he could not explain, but perhaps I might guefs at them: M. M. was written againft many of them ; againft others was K. M. ; and againft a great many I. M. This, I own, puzzled me a little at firft; but, upon confideration, I decyphered them thus ; *ftet*, it feems, was always writ, where *M. M.* was againft the names; and therefore I concluded thofe letters muft mean *miniftry men*, fuch as would be ftaunch friends to the great man, in oppofi-tion to a *greater*, if neceffary, and be always ready to give as much money as fhould be de-fired, in hopes to have a moderate fhare of it properly applied, to encourage merit, and reward faithful fervices.------I could not well explain *K. M.* but fhould have gueffed it ftóod for *king's men*, or *members*, if I had not learnt from my friend, that as many of thefe were to be left out at the new election, as with de-cency could be oppofed. As for *I. M.* I am pretty fure, it was meant for *independent mem-bers*, a ftrange fet of old-fafhioned ruftics, who bring notions of public fpirit, œconomy, and inquiry, with them to parliament, and who, therefore, well deferved, what I found was the cafe, to have the dreadful *dele* invariably put oppofite their names.

F

My

My informant gave me a fpecimen of the, converfation on this curious occafion, between the *great man* and his trufty friends. One of them, for inftance, raifed an objection againft a certain perfon's name being left in the lift, faying, " It was notorioufly known that he vifited at a certain great houfe near ----------."
" Aye, fays *my lord*, that is true ; but he has leave to do fo; and that rather turns to our account; befides, he is quartered for 500 l. a year, on a *North American* contract." ----------
" Pray what does your lordfhip think of fir *Thomas Touchit?*"----" Oh, replied *my lord*, he has leave now and then to vote againft us, and no body knows but myfelf that he has a private penfion."---" *My lord*, (fays another) *Harry Simple* feems to me to be a little fufpicious, and far from a fure man."-------" Don't trouble your head about him, replied his *lord-fhip* ; he is fafe enough ; I faved his uncle about feven years ago, from being hanged. He was a notorious fmuggler, is now very rich, and his nephew *Harry* expects to be his heir ; befides, he is quartered on a patent place, in the cuftoms." " Captain *Wronghead*, fays *my lord*, I doubt will be diftreffed about a qualification ; but he will have no fcruple to fwear to fuch a one, as we can get him ; for he is a very honeft fellow, and will do any thing to ferve his friends."

But I ask pardon, for aiming at ridicule, in treating of an encroachment on the conftitution, which is more properly the object of of indignation. Without pretending, therefore, to fix the exact time, and place, when and where, the above ministerial picture had a real exiſtence, it is with pleaſure I obſerve that ſuch unlimited influence over the electors, who are connected with, and dependent on the crown, cannot be exerted at preſent by any miniſter; becauſe, it muſt then be exerted in direct oppoſition to the declared intention of the *firſt perſonage* in the kingdom, who, we are well aſſured, has abſolutely forbid any of the *public offices* to intermeddle in *elections*.

If the *Roman* generoſity, in proclaiming liberty to the cities of *Greece*, was received with rapture ; with equal rapture, may we well ſuppoſe, have the vaſt body of our fellow ſubjects, whoſe ſtations make them dependent on government, received that unexpected emancipation from miniſterial tyranny, which now leaves them at full liberty to vote according to their own ſentiments ; places them on a level with the reſt of their free-born countrymen, and frees them from the dread of being thought diſreſpectful to the *throne*, though they ſhould be honeſt enough to diſregard the injunctions of the *treaſury* !

That his majeſty has left the ſervants of the crown in this happy ſtate of independence, with regard to elections, is a fact that ſhould be made known, in every corner of the kingdom. And what miniſter dares attempt to fetter them, in oppoſition to this royal declaration ? No ſuch attempt, we may be certain, will be

pub-

publickly made; and, if there be any private efforts made, to defeat his majesty's noble views, of restoring the independence of the constitution, every lover of his country should be watchful to get intelligence of the facts, and to preserve the proofs of them, that proper examples may be made; and that all the nation may know, that subordinate placemen, who refuse to obey a ministerial summons to vote at *elections*, are in less danger of losing their employments, than the minister who shall presume to dictate to them, in opposition to the inclination of the king, and in violation of the independence of the constitution.

History furnishes us with an instance of a people so degenerate, as to reject liberty, when offered.------If the inhabitants of *Great Britain* would avoid the infamy of the old *Cappadocians*, let the patriotism of their generous monarch rouze them from that state of indolent security, and venal dependance on ministers, which hath made but too dangerous a breach in the fortress of liberty. Their common father calls out to them to save themselves, and if there be any spark of public spirit left; if they be not more attached to faction than to the constitution; if they do not think it of less consequence to preserve their country free, than to procure to themselves some dirty advantage for linking in party to destroy it; if such slavish and mercenary principles do not constitute the character of this nation at present; we may now flatter ourselves, to see the

almost

almoft loft powers of the Britifh conftitution reftored to their original vigour.

Here then it will be natural to ask, what are
thofe fteps, which every lover of his country
fhould take, at the enfuing election, that his
majefty's royal intentions may not be defeat-
ed?——The anfwer to this queftion is obvious. Let the country gentlemen, (I mean
gentlemen of every denomination, who have
connection with landed, fixed property)through-
out the kingdom, ftrenuoufly endeavour to get
into Parliament; let them exert their natural
intereft, in their refpective neighbourhoods,
and not allow their boroughs to be ftolen from
them, by mean, low people, who come down
to them, at the time of election, with hands
full of money, and never fee or think of them
afterwards.

Though the public money is no longer to
be employed, in fupport of *court candidates,* it
may well be fuppofed, another fet of oppofers
will ftart up againft the country gentlemen.
The *monied* men of the metropolis will think
this ftagnation of fecret fervice-money, a lucky
incident to get themfelves chofen ; will gladly
offer their fervices to any minifter; and by ad-
vancing each his own money, fupply, in fome
degree, the want of the ufual fund. But, if
the men of property, in every county, would
form themfelves into affociations, to oppofe
every money-jobber, who fhall attempt to invade their boroughs, thefe *merchant adventu-*
ers

ers in politics would foon repent of their electi-
oneering. Loaded as the gentlemen of *England* are, with taxes, and perhaps exhaufted by
former ftruggles at elections, few of them can be
fuppofed to be in fuch circumftances, as to engage fingly with an over-grown *director*, who,
inftead of paying any thing to the public burthens, is annually increafing his capital, by
preying upon the neceffities of the ftate. But
what no individual is equal to, on his own bottom, fupported by the joint intereft, and by a
joint purfe of all his neighbours, will eafily and
cheaply be accomplifhed.

If our houfe of commons is to be filled with
men who are in trade, and who get themfelves
elected, only to be in the way of their trade ;
the *contracts*, the *jobs*, the *fubfcriptions*, the *loans*,
the *remittances*, &c. &c. with which a minifter
can benefit them, are fuch a temptation to
them, to affift in involving the nation in dangerous projects, and ruinous expence, that I
know not whether we have moft reafon to dread
a majority of greedy *ftock-holders*, or of indigent
placemen, for our reprefentatives. Every one,
therefore, who wifhes well to his country, who
would hope to fee a parliament attached to the
king and the conftitution, and not fubfervient
to minifterial influence and direction, naturally
will turn his eyes on the country gentlemen of
England, at this critical conjuncture, and call
upon them to exert themfelves with vigour, to
wreft the honour of being reprefentatives of
the people, from a fet of men, who either
havo

have no *property* at all, or fuch a fort of property, as bears no fhare in the expences of the ftate.

If the fhutting up of the exchequer, and the emancipation of placemen, are ftrong encouragements to the gentlemen of property, and great eftates, to attempt getting themfelves chofen at the next election, the peculiar fituation of the kingdom, at this juncture, is another moft powerful motive to animate them to the conduct I recommend.

Every great and national object, that can deferve the attention of the prefent age, and fix the happinefs or mifery of this country, to lateft pofterity, muft neceffarily come under the confideration of the next parliament.-------- Difeafes in the body politic, equally with thofe in the natural body, have their crifis; and whoever fits down to ruminate on the prefent ftate and fituation of this kingdom, if he has any fhare of political fagacity, will fee but too much reafon to conclude, that by a train of meafures, adopted too long in former times of peace, the conftitution has been undermined; and by a wantonnefs of expence in former wars, and in the prefent, we are, at laft, brought almoft to the very brink of a precipice, which imagination can fcarcely furvey, without horror.

To recover this conftitution before it be entirely loft, to inquire into the caufes of the
increafe

increafe of our immenfe debt, and to devife means of leffening it, muft, therefore, be the great object of the enfuing parliament, other-wife ruin and deftruction will at laft overtake us.

But can this be a feafon for fuch inquiries ? When all the attention of parliament muft be confined to furnifh frefh fums to defray the amazing expence of a confuming war, can this be a time to fet on foot plans of reformation ? ⸺No, furely ;⸺and while I confefs the fact, I lament it as an addition to our mif-fortunes. Till peace be happily reftored, no-thing can be done to fave the nation ; and eve-ry day that peace is deferred, will increafe the difficulty of faving it. Like a prodigal heir, who fpends annually four times more than the real income of his eftate, we muft, if our ex-pences continue, at laft be unable to find fecu-rity for a frefh mortgage, or a fund to pay frefh intereft. In this alarming firuation, it is the only confolation to us, that the bravery of our troops by fea and land, has humbled the power, deftroyed the trade, and ruined the navy of our enemy ; and that though *France* is ftill but too able to cope with us on the continent of *Europe*, with which we are unhappily connect-ed, we may hope from the multiplied defola-tions of the poor country, now the feat of war, that it will be impoffible much longer to conti-nue the horrid fcene of bloodfhed.

It

It is not therefore an unreasonable presumption, that the first sessions of a new parliament, instead of laying on fresh burthens, and adding to our already intolerable debts, will be more agreeably employed in deliberations concerning the terms of peace.-------With regard to these I shall only observe, that though it will require all the abilities of our ablest negociators, to settle the jarring interests of the powers at war, we may be confident that the essential interests of *Great-Britain* will be taken care of. Blessed with the best of princes that ever filled a throne, who, *born and educated amongst us, and glorying in the name of Briton*, has no object so dear to him as the happiness of his country, ------- we need not doubt that he will forward the much wished for, and much wanted return of peace ; and when once he has extricated the nation from that distress in which he found us involved, that he will co-operate with an honest and independent parliament, to restore an almost lost constitution.

Aspice venturo lætantur ut omnia sæclo !
Jam nova progenies !   Virg.

Had the long peace that succeeded, from the treaty of Utrecht, to the breaking out of the Spanish war in 1738, been properly employed, in lessening our debts, and reforming abuses connected with them, we should not, at this time of day, have had any gloomy apprehensions concerning their consequences. But, by an uninterrupted course of borrowing, a total ne-

G   glect

gle&t of paying off, and by a corrupt want of œconomy in fpending, we have, at laft, been funk into fuch an abyfs of diftrefs, that if providence had not raifed up a prince, who fcorns and renounces thofe arts of government, which have been too fatally put in practice, by corrupt adminiftrations, our conftitution, nay our very exiftence as an independent kingdom, feemed verging to annihilation.

An honeft and independent parliament, feconded, nay, rather excited by the patriotifm and virtue which now adds frefh luftre to majefty, will do wonders ftill towards faving us. Should the national debt (at once the caufe and effect of the languifhing ftate of conftitutional freedom) be fuffered to remain at its prefent enormous height, we need not be furprized if, like a bubble filled with air, it burft of itfelf, as the *South Sea fcheme* formerly did. And if this fhould happen, let any true Englifhman think what extenfive deftruction muft be fpread over the whole kingdom. Thoufands, nay millions, muft be brought to immediate and irremediable ruin. And what rage, what flaughter, what anarchy this may occafion, it is better for us to try to prevent, than to defcribe. Credit is a thing of fo delicate a nature, that the leaft diftruft may occafion the total lofs of it : when that is gone, all finks at once with it ; but the hand of the legiflature, by feeling the pulfe of the nation, may apply fuch parliamentary remedies, as may fupport credit, and think of fome fcheme for a regular, though flow payment, of our debt.

One

One circumstance alone is too alarming not to be carefully attended to: foreigners have got a vast share of this debt into their hands. Perhaps our amazing loans of late years never could have been filled, had not annual millions of foreign money poured in upon us. But if this has been a temporary relief, and enabled us to go on with the war, think how it will distress us in time of full peace. If we suppose foreigners to be in possession of thirty millions in our stocks, (much of which has been bought in at twenty-five and thirty *per cent.* discount) the interest of this money will drain the kingdom of perhaps a million and a half every year. And when once it happens, that foreigners draw more from this country for their interest in our funds, than we gain from them, by balance of trade, she shall be actually in a state of incurable consumption, and the whole enquiry will be, how long the patient may be able to drag out a miserable existence.

What scheme can possibly be devised, to lessen the intolerable burthen, it is not for me to determine: but this every one may foresee, that much will depend on the future state of our commerce. If by an increase of that (an increase we may reasonably hope for, if our America and West-India colonies are not checked by French encroachments) the produce of the *sinking fund* is augmented, the religious, and inviolable application of this annual sum (without which no plan of payment can ever succeed)

G 2   will,

will, in cafe we be fo happy as to enjoy a laft-
ing peace, eafe this poor country of great part
of that load under which fhe now finks, and
under the weight of which, I fear, it will be
impoffible for it ever to rife again, to make efforts to fave itfelf from the future attempts of
our inveterate and infidious enemy.

But if the increafe of commerce, and the religious application of the *finking fund*, will be a
foundation for devifing fome fcheme of reduc-
ing our debt; under fuch a prince as we now
have, and with fuch a parliament as we now
wifh to have, what may we not alfo expect, by
a due attention to national œconomy ?----Were
a minute enquiry to be made into the unneceffary expence in collecting our revenue, and into the infinite and abominable abufes and frauds
that are practifed, in almoft every branch of
it, I make not the leaft doubt, that fuch an annual faving could be made, as would be of the
higheft confequence in the prefent diftreffed
circumftances of the ftate. Want of œconomy,
and culpable profufion, will foon diforder the
affairs of the richeft perfon; but one whofe
eftate is loaded with tenfold mortgages, muft
be a madman, who goes on in a courfe of wan-
ton riot, and fuffers himfelf to be preyed upon
by a fwarm of unneceffary, difhoneft, and ex-
penfive domeftics. Were an honeft parliament
to look into the management of our *cuftom-
houfe*, and there to obferve, that there is fcarcely
a fingle place that is not executed by deputies,

if

if not by the deputies of deputies ; were they to carry on their inquiry through the many offices that have the care of every other part of our income ; they would, without abolishing one place really useful, or diminishing one salary more than it ought to be, make retrenchments that would, in a course of few years, ease us of the load of millions.

The single article of unnecessary pensions, which times of corruption have so amazingly increased, would be an annual fund, to enable a virtuous monarch, oppressed by his greedy courtiers, to lend a most effectual assistance towards the glorious work of saving the state. Such hath been the fashion of the times, that pensions have been asked, for every reason but the single one, for which they ought to be given,---the indigence of the pensioner ; nay, they have been increased, in proportion as the persons who obtained them were opulent. To such an unhappy state hath the crown been reduced, that almost every *great man*, who is turned out of employment, or who retires from it, though he is master of a noble estate, and has added to his wealth by his places, thinks he has a right to be put upon the list of *pensioners*, and to have thousands a year settled upon him for life. In order to expose the absurdity of all such extravagant profusion of the public money, consider how many persons are rendered miserable, by this seeming piece of good nature? What loads we entail upon our unhappy

unhappy posterity, whose teeth will be set on edge by the sour grapes their great, great grand-fathers have tasted, to feed one luxurious and expensive man?----- If the pension be 4000 l. a year, four thousand midling families must contribute to bear his evtravagance: twenty shillings a year must be continued on 4000 houses, to enable him to make a birth-day dinner, or to stake his thousands at a Pharaoh table. For the future let us denominate pensions, by the name of, taxes; and say that my lord such a one runs away with the *fortieth* part of the *salt duty*; that another spends about *two thirds* a year, out of the tax on *tallow*; and that a third drinks prodigiously deep, from the severe additional duty on *Porter's ale*.

But, besides devising means of payment, an honest, and independent parliament will find it incumbent on them, to enquire immediately into the first rise, and the rapid progress of our present amazingly *multiplied* incumbrances. ,

If we should take up the consideration of this important affair, from the year 1716, when the sinking fund was first established, or from any other later period, we shall find that scarcely any of the debt which we now groan under, has ever been accounted for; and I fancy it will be extremely difficult ever to account for it properly to the public. Not one, perhaps, for many years, of the money-offices, has ever thought of passing any account ; and a *paymaster,* who has been dead some years, when he was asked how he intended to pass some intricate accounts, had the honesty, or rather the effrontery to own, with a smile, that he never designed they should be passed. I wish this may not be a principle adopted by our public officers in general, who without fear of inquiry, or censure, daily suffer most amazing sums to pass through their hands, which I am sure can never be accounted for by the regular ways of the Exchequer. How is it possible, for instance, to produce satisfactory vouchers for the incredible amount of our German contingencies? Can the confused expences of our West India, and American expeditions, ever be sufficiently explained? ---- And surely it is highly unreasonable that privy seals should be granted, to indemnify those who are accountable for the expenditure of such sums; at least till the *chaos* has been brought into some order, by a parliamentary examination.

But nothing will be more necessary, when the honest days of serious inquiry commence, than to sift to the bottom the state of the navy accounts. For the management of this branch of our service has been as extravagant, as it is little understood. I almost blush to mention, (but the fact is too certain) that in this department particularly, estimates seem to have been annually laid before parliament, merely for the sake of form, and without the least intention of adapting the expence of the fleet to the supplies

plies asked and obtained. And this has now been practifed fo long, without controul, that parliaments have had but little or nothing left for them to do, with regard to this great article, but to find out funds to anfwer navy debts of *four or five millions*, which, from time to time, they are told have been incurred, by the *fiats* of a navy or victualling board. But the affumed authority of fuch fubordinate offices, in loading the nation with debts without the knowledge of parliament, is not the only point that requires to be regulated; fomething muft be done to introduce œconomy, the want of which, in the affairs of our marine at prefent, we have but too much to lament. Can it be furprizing, that our navy debt fo amazingly increafes, when we reflect that the public buys its ftores, its provifions, hires its tranfports, and makes its contracts, at a monftrous difadvantage? Every one in the leaft acquainted with *the courfe of the navy*, muft own the truth of this moft melancholy fact; and, therefore, it will be highly worthy to be enquired into, and to be remedied by a diligent and honeft *committee*, to whofe care, we truft, the enfuing parliament will refer the ftate of our navy, which of late years hath been fo copious a fource of incumbrances. And while fuch an enquiry will be of infinite ufe, in preventing future unneceffary expences, in fitting out our fleets, may we not alfo hope it will be of real fervice to the public, to be able to calculate how many *millions* have been expended

pended to refit our fhips, fhattered by braving
the feafons, without blocking up the enemy, in
the Bay of Bifcay ; and to maintain our numerous fquadrons, fo long employed *in hedging in
the cuckow*, in the river Vilaine.

There is one article in the accounts of the
navy, of a very extraordinary nature. If any
one will look into them, he will find that very
confiderable fums remain in the hands of *feveral right honourable* gentlemen, who *formerly* have
been treafurers. Thefe fums, indeed, are faid
to be retained till they may be able to pafs their
accounts, and to pay for the charges of paffing
them. But ought it to be permitted, to lock
up for many years, fo much public money, at
a time when we are obliged to pay off one bit
of paper with another, and are reduced to the
comfortable fituation of fending *navy bills* into
the market, at a difcount of above ten *per cent?*
--Befides, may I ask where does that money lye
at intereft ? and who is to have the advantage
of it ? Thefe are queftions very proper to be
asked ; and as I have before taken notice, that
it has been ufual to give confiderable penfions,
to every one turned out of employment, I hope
that, at leaft, *treafurers of the navy*, who have
perhaps fifteen or twenty thoufand pounds of
public money circulating in Change Alley, or
fixed in mortgages, for many years after they
have ceafed to have the place, will be thought
to have no claim to the king's bounty as pen-
fioners.---Happy had it been for this country, if
all our public officers had been animated by the

H   fame

same disinterested spirit, which has distinguish-
ed, in so remarkable a manner, the character
of one gentleman; who once enjoyed the employment we now speak of! who quitted it,
perhaps from a mistaken, but certainly from a
generous delicacy of sentiment, worthier of
praise than of imitation; and whom we now see
retiring from the senatorial *chair* he has filled
with so much dignity, for above thirty years,
like another *Cincinnatus*; superior to the glare
of proffered titles; rich in the applause of every honest man, and in the pleasing feelings of
self-approbation,----a reward that the patriot a-
lone can enjoy, and which accumulated treasures
cannot purchase.

The sums retained by some late treasurers
of the navy, (on whom, however, I mean to
throw no particular blame) call to my mind
another article very little known, and hardly
understood. I mean the state of the money
due to the *marines*, who served during the last
war. No account of this has been given, I
think, ever since 1746. What then is become
of the money? It is well known it has been issued by parliament,----and it is well known that
the poor officers and men, of the respective re-
giments, have never received it.---If they could
not make up their regimental accounts in form,
were not such persons the proper objects to be
assisted by privy seals? Or if *they* were not to
be so much favored, why, after so many years,
has not the money in question been applied to
the public service, and not left in the hands of a
few

few griping agents and fecretaries, who have
but too many other means of preying on the
public?

But, before the miferable condition of our fi-
nances can be effectually inquired into, befides
appointment of *felect*, nay *fecret committees* in the
houfe of commons, the public flatters itfelf,
that the wifdom of the legiflature will go farther, and erect, by act of parliament, a *commif-
fion for taking and ftating the public accounts:* the
commiffioners to be chofen from amongft the
greateft and ableft men of the kingdom, of
both houfes, or otherwife; to continue for years
together (if it fhould be neceffary) to fit where,
and at what time they pleafe; affifted by the
ableft clerks they can find; and vefted with unlimited power over all the public offices; to
fcrutinize into all the money tranfactions that
have paffed of late years; to make reports, from
time to time, to parliament, of the progrefs
they may make in cleanfing the *Augean ftable*,
and to call for parliamentary cenfures, if neceffary. The public debt is a wound that muft
be probed to the bottom: not with a furious
and malicious intent to fearch for, and to find
out delinquents, but with an honeft view, to
fave a finking conftitution, and the liberties of
this country. But if any delinquents fhould be
found out, though I could wifh every thing
was done with as little feverity as poffible, furely it is better that fome few of the moft culpable fhould be fingled out, as they ought to be,
rather than that the nation, by a general bank-

H 2 rupicy,

ruptcy, fhould be thrown into a moft calamitous
defolation. And may we not reafonably hope
that an inftance or two, of fevere animadverfion
on domeftic mifmanagements will, for the future, imprint this important leffon on the mind
of every one, whofe office makes him accountable to the ftate, that no connections are ftrong
eno: gh to fcreen *corruption*, and that *public rob-
bery* is as dangerous as it is criminal?

And now, after enumerating the above particulars which have occurred to me, on taking
a curfory view of our prefent fituation, it cannot furely be neceffary, before I conclude, to
mention any more facts (though many more
might be mentioned) to convince my readers,
how little is known of the real application of the
immenfe fums voted of late years by parliament;
and how neceffary it will be to have a day of
parli r tary reckoning for all thefe matters.
The diftreffes of the ftate point it out; the voice
of the nation loudly demands it; and, what is
moft confiderable, we have a fovereign, who
renounces the mean arts of venal adminiftration, by which alone the much wifhed for inquiry can be obftructed.----Motions for reforming
any abufe, or redreffing any grievance, will
ftand but little chance of fuccceding, if oppofed
by the crown. But when the firft advances towards this reformation, when the firft fteps towards this redrefs are made voluntarily by the
crown, nothing remains to infure their fuccefs,
but fuch a conduct in the people, as may fhew,
that they are not altogether unworthy of fuch

a prince, and of such valuable privileges, calls upon them to preserve....

Let every *honest man*, therefore, exert self at the approaching elections, that a ment may be chosen of *honest men*; of independent fortunes, but loyal principles whose inclination it may be to supp throne and the constitution, against m insolence, and corrupt administration. if the landed gentlemen of *England* duty, on this important occasion; if prove, as they ought to do, the adva generously offered to them, by the ch to the undue influence of governr rupted as the morals of the electors, ny of our boroughs are, by a long stitution, there is a fair and reasonable prospect, that we may, upon the whole, see such an assembly of representatives, as will co-operate with his majesty, in carrying his gracious purposes into execution.

I know too well, that there is not wanting amongst us, a set of men who affect to ridicule every attempt to reform the nation, and to restore the constitution, as a wild *Eutopian* scheme, and impossible to be put in practice; nay, who (as far as they dare venture to do it) try to render all amiable and virtuous inclinations contemptible, even in the *highest person*, where they are most eminently conspicuous.--- If candidates of this sort offer themselves to represent us, we cannot surely be so infatuated as

to

...gate to them a trust, which, we may be ..., they mean to betray. By trusting men ... profligate principles, on former occasi- ... foundations of our present distress were. ... *representatives* of a different character, ... be chosen, if we would ... or hope to ... from the dregs of *corruption*, into vir- ... and constitutional *independence*.

F I N I S.